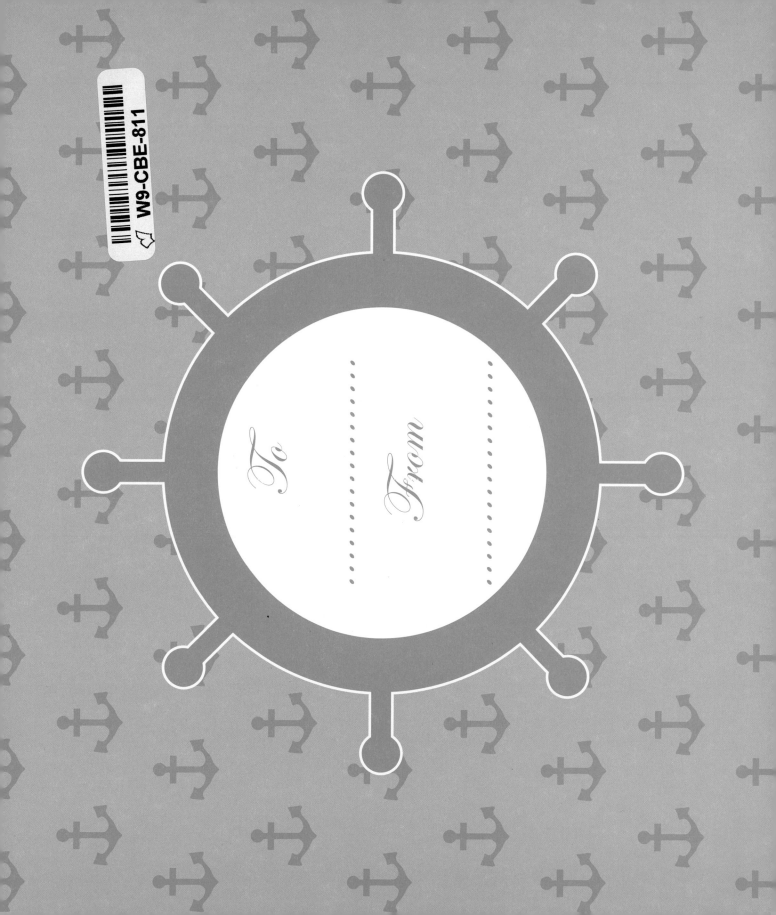

To

From

Peter the Cruise Ship

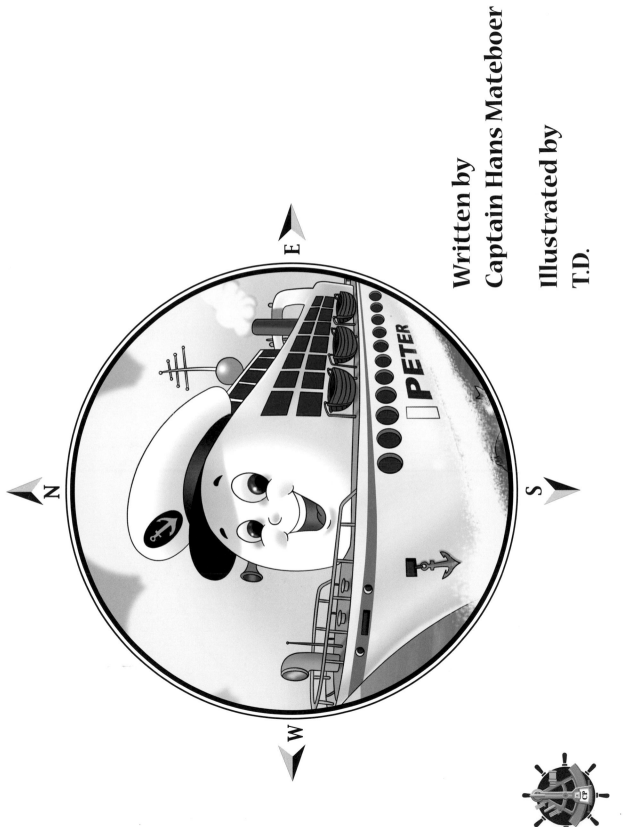

Written by
Captain Hans Mateboer

Illustrated by
T.D.

Peter the Cruise Ship travels all over the world and has many adventures on the oceans.

PETER

Most ships are
Peter's friends.
He meets many
of them whenever
he is out to sea.

3

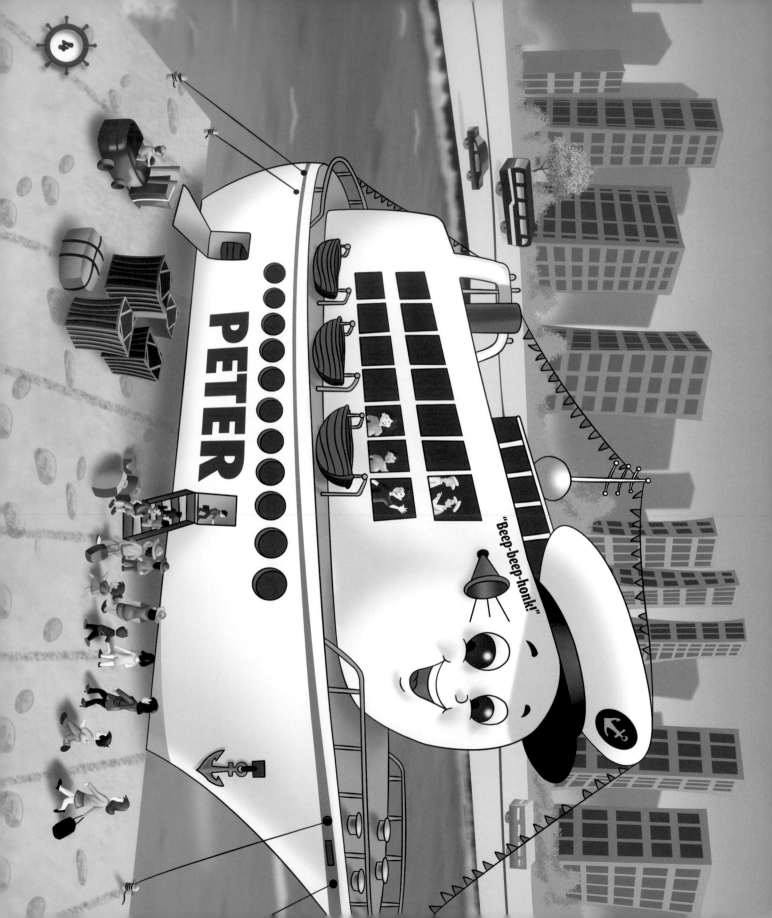

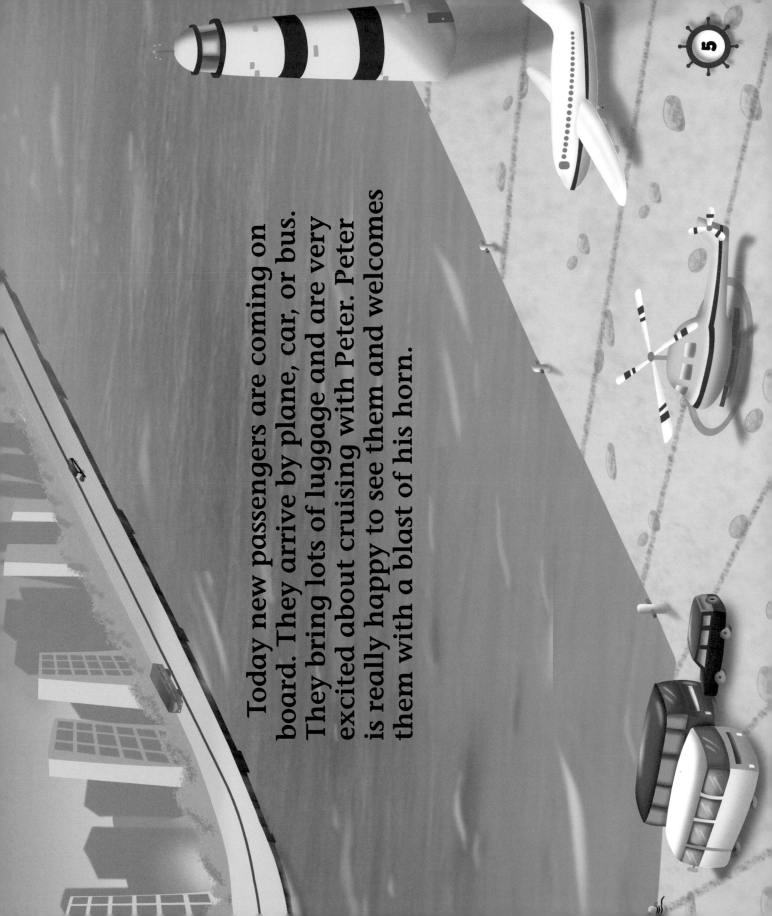

Today new passengers are coming on board. They arrive by plane, car, or bus. They bring lots of luggage and are very excited about cruising with Peter. Peter is really happy to see them and welcomes them with a blast of his horn.

The captain steers the ship from the bridge. He tells the sailors to be very careful. Peter is glad to have a good captain.

"Aye-aye, Sir!"

Deep down below in the engine room, the engineer starts Peter's motors. The propellers start to turn.

"Chug–a–chug–a, chug–a–chug–a!
Chug–a–chug–a, chug–a–chug–a!"

"Clang, clang!"

Peter blows his whistle at the other ships. They watch as Peter sails from the harbor. The passengers wave goodbye to their friends ashore.

"Ayugaa, ayugaa!"

Peter carefully steers toward the ocean. The red and the green buoys warn him of shallow water.

"Ring-a-ling, ring-a-ling!"

"Beep-beep!"

"Toot-toot"

"Harumph!"

Push

"Putter-putter-
putter-putter."

"Huff 'n' puff,
huff 'n' puff."

SLICK

RUSTY

GULP

"Chug-a-luga,
chug-a-luga."

On the ocean, Peter meets his friends.
Slick is a container ship. Rusty is an old cargo ship.
Gulp is an oil tanker.

But Peter and the other ships stay away from Push the tugboat. Push always bumps into the other ships and is grumpy all the time.

Peter and his friends travel all over the world. They visit Europe, Japan, China, India, Africa, Australia, and South America.

North America

South America

PETER

RUSTY

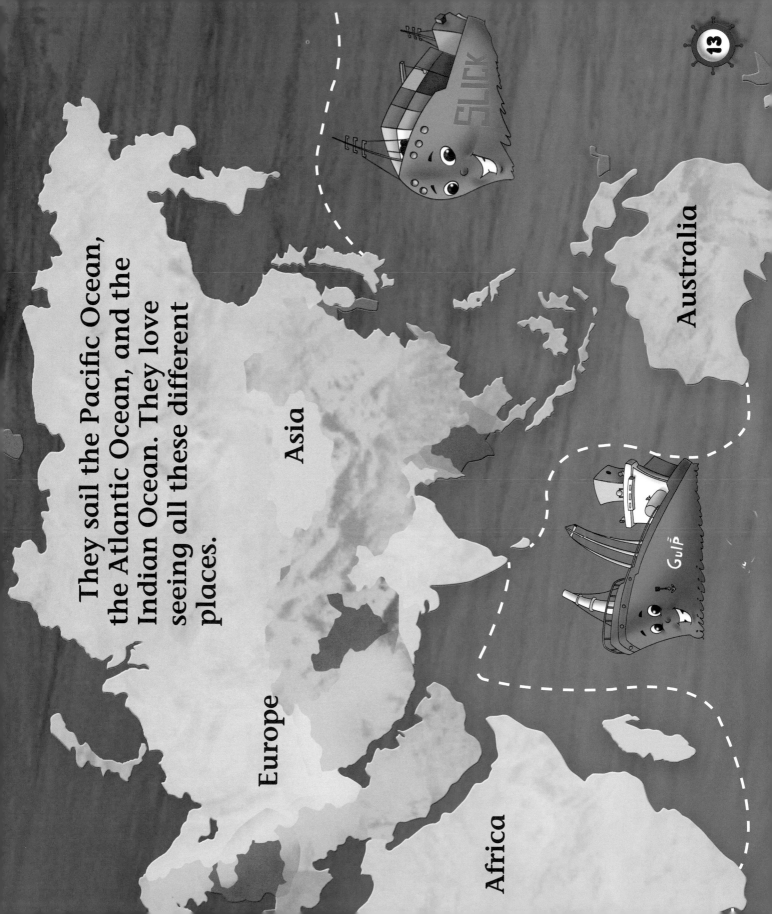

They sail the Pacific Ocean, the Atlantic Ocean, and the Indian Ocean. They love seeing all these different places.

Asia

Europe

Africa

Australia

SLICK

Gulp

At night, Peter is guided by the stars. He knows the other ships by their red, white, and green lights.

"Twinkle, twinkle!"

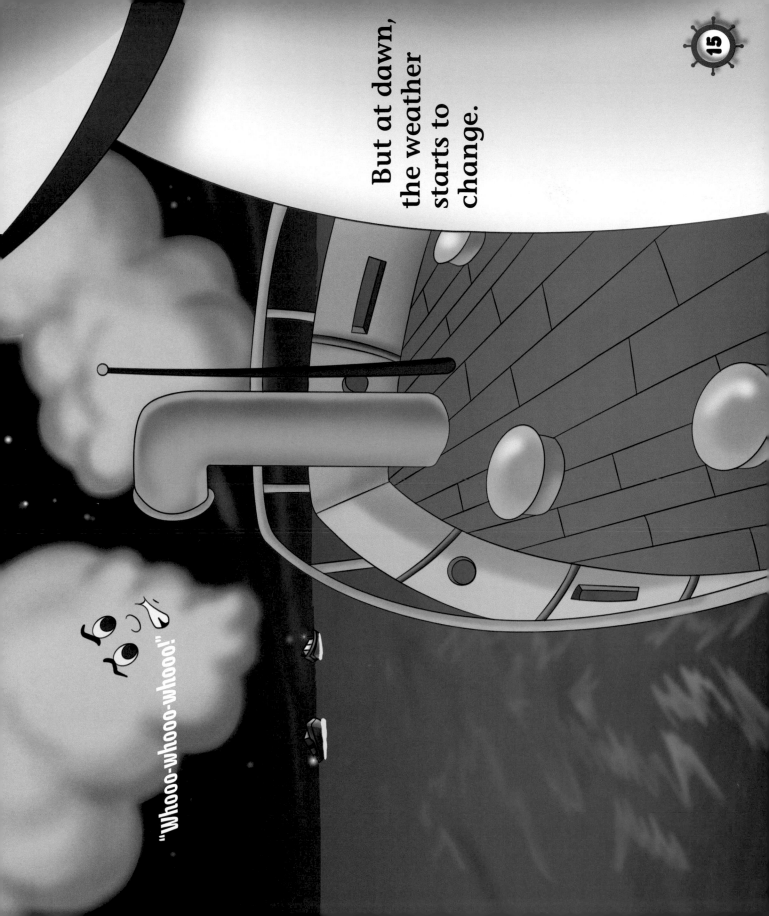

The sea is wild. The waves are high and rough. The wind howls. There is thunder and lightning. All the ships are tossed around. Peter knows he has to stay away from the rocks.

"Whoosh, crackle, boom!"

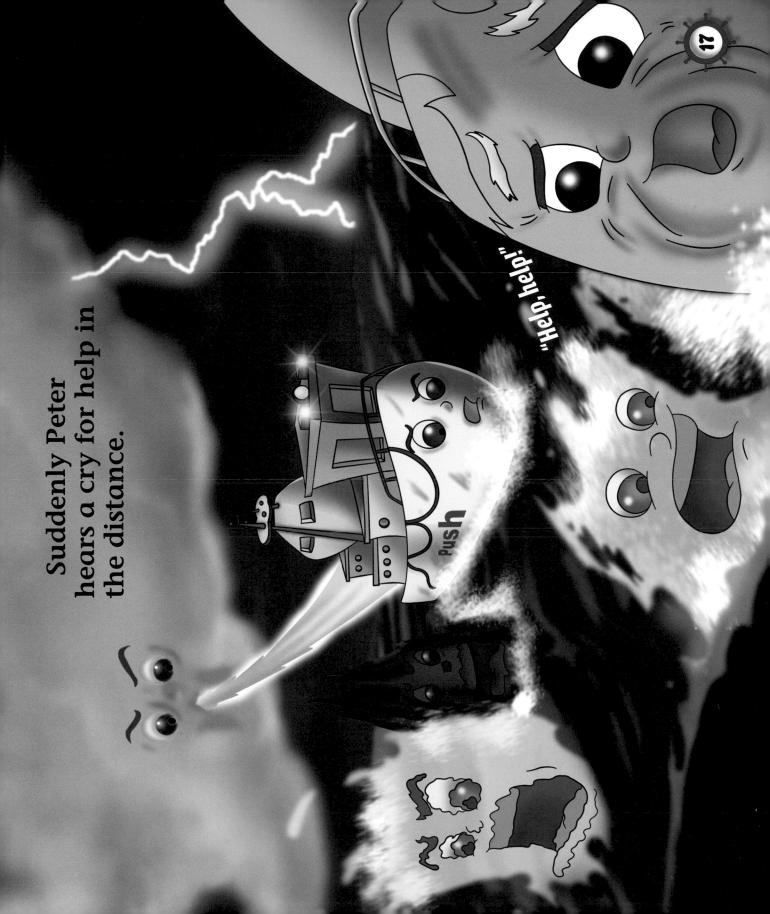

Suddenly Peter hears a cry for help in the distance.

"Help, help!"

Push

It's Rusty. He can't handle the big waves any longer. "Help!" Rusty shouts. He is very afraid.

Peter sails as fast as he can to rescue Rusty, and so does Push, the tugboat.

Sometimes, the waves and the sea foam cover Peter completely, but he keeps going. Peter reaches Rusty first. Push arrives too. "We'll save you!" Peter shouts.

"Crash, swoosh, bang!"

"Hold on," says Push.
He throws a rope and
bumps into Rusty.
"Sorry," says Push.

But Rusty doesn't mind the bump.
He knows Push is doing his job.
"Thank you," Rusty says
while Push steadies him and
pulls him to safety.
Peter is glad they are now
all friends—Push too!

"Whew!"

"Thump, bump!"

Push

Push tows Rusty to a harbor where they are greeted by Tim the old tugboat and his little son Teddie. They will tow Rusty to the shipyard for repairs.

"Chug-chug, sputter, sputter!"

Finally Peter arrives at his first port. It is a beautiful tropical island. He is in such a hurry to let down his anchor, that he drops it on Fluke, the whale!

"Thump!"

Fluke is having breakfast with his family. "Ouch!" cries Fluke, "What hit me?"

At the end of the day,
it is time for Peter to leave.
Fluke is still angry. His head
is very sore. Peter feels bad and
wants to make up with Fluke.

Peter knows he
has to apologize.
"I'm sorry, Fluke.
I was in a hurry
because I was late
after helping Rusty,"
he explains.
"That's okay,"
says Fluke. "We
all make mistakes."

Finally, Peter arrives back in his home port. Grumble the bridge complains. "You're too tall, you will hit me!" So Peter sails very carefully under Grumble.

"Clang-clang!"

"Beep-beep!"

"Honk!"

GulP

RUSTY

All of Peter's friends are there—
including Push—to tell the
stories of their adventures at sea!

The next day Peter leaves the harbor again.
He is ready for new adventures.

"Goodbye!" he shouts as he sets sail.

CPSIA Compliance Information: Batch #0210.
For further information contact RJ Communications,
NY, NY, 1-800-621-2556

ISBN: 978-0-9759487-1-2
www.captainspublishing.com
Published by Captain's Publishing
Print in the United States of America